Baby squirrels are called kittens.

The name squirrel means *shade tail*.

Squirrels also use their tails as blankets.

Squirrels love eating nuts and berries.

This book belongs to:

_____

All Ladybird books are available at most bookshops,
supermarkets and newsagents, or can be ordered direct from:
Ladybird Postal Sales
PO Box 133 Paignton TQ3 2YP England
Telephone: (+44) 01803 554761
Fax: (+44) 01803 663394

A catalogue record for this book is available
from the British Library

Published by Ladybird Books Ltd
A subsidiary of the Penguin Group
A Pearson Company

Text © Geraldine Taylor MCMXCVIII
Illustrations © LADYBIRD BOOKS LTD MCMXCVIII

LADYBIRD and the device of a Ladybird are trademarks of
Ladybird Books Ltd Loughborough Leicestershire UK

The Great Squirrel Hunt

by Geraldine Taylor
illustrated by Lesley Smith

Chatterbox the squirrel sang as he skipped from branch to branch, his feathery tail flowing behind him like a bright red shadow.

> *"See me scamper, watch me hop!*
> *See me run right to the top…!"*

"There goes Chatterbox," said the other squirrels, "boasting again!"

"He says he's the most daring squirrel in the world," said his sister, Baby Bush. "*And* the cleverest."

"And now he says he's going to win our game of hide and seek," said his brother, Little Tufts. "He says he's found the best place to hide in the *whole of* Acorn Wood!"

"We'll see," said their mother.

Chatterbox wanted to hide first. He waited
for the other squirrels by the old tree stump,
singing,

> "I'm off to hide, count one, two, three.
> Hunt high and low – you won't find me!"

Suddenly Baby Bush jumped out and flicked her
tail at him.

"Yes we *will*, Chatterbox," she said. "We know
all the hiding places in this wood, *too*!"

"Not *this* one!" boasted Chatterbox, laughing.

The other squirrels covered their eyes and Chatterbox scuttled off as though the wind were chasing him. He knew exactly where he wanted to go. Down to the old railway station at the edge of the wood.

Dozens of people were there when he arrived, boarding a long, shining train.

Daring and reckless, Chatterbox dashed onto the train, too. "They won't find me in *here*!" he chuckled.

Chatterbox leapt over laps and shoulders. Ladies shrieked as he scampered over their heads. Hats and newspapers scattered everywhere. Children laughed and pointed. Hands reached out to catch him, and someone pulled his tail.

Chatterbox jumped up to the parcel shelf and huddled behind baskets and bags, his heart thumping. Suddenly the train hissed, lurched forward and began its long race through the countryside.

Chatterbox peeped out of the window and saw that his wood was already a long, long way away. What had he done? He hated the noisy clickety-clack of the train, and he crept inside a basket to hide.

By now the other squirrels were hunting for Chatterbox.

"Perhaps he *does* know the best hiding place in the whole of Acorn Wood," said Baby Bush.

But Mother Squirrel was worried...

At last, the train stopped and the doors opened. Someone lifted Chatterbox's basket down. He scampered out of it and looked around with astonishment.

Here was the biggest blue pond he had ever seen, stretching far into the distance.

Chatterbox was so surprised that he forgot all about his wood and the game of hide and seek.

While Chatterbox was gazing at the sea, Mother Squirrel was organising a desperate hunt for him in the forest. The message was passed from squirrel to squirrel: "Find Chatterbox, find Chatterbox…"

They searched to the top of every tree and looked in every birds' nest. Baby Bush peered into every woodpecker hole. It was the greatest squirrel hunt in the history of Acorn Wood.

There was no sign of Chatterbox.

Chatterbox was hot and thirsty. He held his tail over his head like a sunshade and tiptoed through the strange yellow sand towards the sea for a drink. He took one sip and a big wave rolled up and drenched him! The water tasted very nasty, but Chatterbox was beginning to enjoy his adventure.

"I wish Baby Bush and all the others could see me now," he said, hopping from rock to rock. He stared into a pool, perching on a small stone to take a closer look. Suddenly the stone moved sideways and Chatterbox fell into the water! A monstrous claw reached out towards him…

Chatterbox was terrified. He scrambled out of the pool, slithered over a slippery rock and dashed back up the beach. There, right in front of him, was the basket he'd used in the train.

With great relief, Chatterbox squeezed inside and curled up tightly. He didn't feel very brave any more.

After a while, he felt the basket move and sway like the branches of a tree. He was back in the train! Before long the basket was carried outside. Chatterbox jumped out and began to race up the moonlit valley towards Acorn Wood.

At the edge of the trees he stopped. The screech of an owl reminded him that he should be safely in the treetops by now, with all the other squirrels. The foxes, owls and badgers were hunting in the valley – danger was all around him.

"I'm the most daring squirrel in all the world," Chatterbox said, uncertainly, "and now I am going home!" He shivered and started to sing softly, to give himself courage.

"See me scamper, watch me hop!
See me run right to the top…!"

A twig snapped behind him.

Without stopping to look round, Chatterbox raced into the wood, up his tree and straight into the paws of his astonished mother.

As the stars came out between the treetops, Chatterbox curled his tail round himself like a blanket. Baby Bush, who was on a branch nearby, heard him singing:

> *"I'm off to hide, count one, two, three.*
> *Hunt high and low…"*

But Chatterbox didn't finish his song. He was fast asleep and dreaming…